For Uncle Tim and Auntie Sheila, who always wrote to tell me when the swallows had arrived back with them – A.W.

For my big brother, Rich – J.B.

First published in Great Britain in 2024 by Andersen Press Ltd., 20 Vauxhall Bridge Road, London SW1V 2SA, UK • Vijverlaan 48, 3062 HL Rotterdam, Nederland.
 Printed and bound in China.

1 3 5 7 9 10 8 6 4 2

British Library Cataloguing in Publication Data available. ISBN 978 1 83913 375 6

MIX
Paper from responsible sources
FSC® C104723

Anna Wilson Jenny Bloomfield

Be Back Soon

Andersen Press

Every Sunday Bibi and his little brother Mo went to the lake together. They loved to watch the hornbills and the storks and the ibis and the lilac-breasted roller birds.

But best of all they loved to watch the swallows.
"Bet I spot the first one!" said Mo.
"Bet I do!" said Bibi. "Race you!"

Then –
"A swallow!" cried Mo.
"I see it!" said Bibi. "I see its forked tail."

They watched the ink-blue swallow,
chirruping and chirping,
dipping and diving,
skimming the surface of the
shining silver lake.

"It's chasing insects on the wing," said Bibi.
"Look at me, I'm flying too!"
"Don't fly away from me!" Mo shouted.

"I have to go away soon, remember?" said Bibi.
Mo sighed. "I don't like it when you go."
"I have to go north to work," said Bibi. "Just like the swallows have to go north to have their chicks."
"When will you be back?" asked Mo.

Bibi smiled. "When the flowers bloom again.
When the sun shines. In the summer."
"Like the swallows?" Mo asked.
"Yes. I'll follow them," said Bibi.

“When you’re
missing me, think
of me flying with
the swallows.

*We’ll soar over the tops
of the mountains.*

*We’ll fly over the big-beaked
hornbills and the
long-legged storks.*

Over the noisy ibis and the lilac-breasted roller birds.

Over the eagles and the buzzards,

the hawks and the falcons and the kestrels.

We'll whizz across the tips of the trees in the jungles. The monkeys will swing from the branches below. The snakes will slither along the forest floor.

The grasslands will spread out, wide and wild beneath us.
Even the giraffes won't be able to reach us.

And then we'll cross the ocean.
Dolphins will jump and twirl and play.
Whales and seals will swim and dive and fish.
And we'll fly above them all.

The swallows know exactly where to go.

And they know how to get back,
just like I know how to get back to you.

When the swallows get to the north, they'll build neat little nests.

They'll lay their eggs and hatch their chicks.

Then, when the
summer's over
in the north,
and the chicks are
big and strong,

they'll learn to fly.

They'll make their
long journey back
here to our lake.

Across the cities

and the roads
and the railways.

Across the oceans

and the grasslands

and the jungle.

Back over the tops of the mountains.
Back home to our lake.
When the flowers bloom again.
When the sun shines. In the summer."

Then, one morning –
"A swallow!" cried Mo.

It soared high in the sky.
It looped-the-loop.
It swooped down low.

And as it turned in the sky,
Mo noticed something else . . .

"Bibi!" he cried.
"I told you I'd come back," said Bibi.
"Like the swallows," said Mo.

"Yes," said Bibi. "I
followed the swallows.
All the way back
home to you."

The swallows fly nearly ten thousand kilometres from the southern hemisphere to the northern hemisphere! They make this long journey because when it gets colder in the south, there are fewer insects for them to eat, so they have to fly north to find more food.

As the swallows fly, they eat *insects*, such as horseflies and bluebottles.

Sometimes they stop on telegraph wires, to rest their wings and sleep.

When they get to the north, they build little nests or re-use nests they have built before. They lay their eggs and hatch their chicks.

Then, when the summer's over in the north, and the chicks have learnt to fly, the swallows will make their journey back to the southern hemisphere to find insects to eat. Ten thousand kilometres, all over again.